In loving memory of Ladye Zilpah Peterson and in honour
of my precious granddaughter, Nami Elizabeth McGee – M M

For Io and Tam – G S

LITTLE TIGER PRESS
An imprint of Magi Publications
1 The Coda Centre, 189 Munster Road, London SW6 6AW
www.littletigerpress.com

First published in Great Britain 2010
This edition published 2011

Text copyright © Marni McGee 2010
Illustrations copyright © Gavin Scott 2010
Marni McGee and Gavin Scott have asserted their rights
to be identified as the author and illustrator of this work
under the Copyright, Designs and Patents Act, 1988

A CIP catalogue record for this book is available
from the British Library

Printed in China • LTP/1400/0201/0511

10 9 8 7 6 5 4 3 2

This Little Tiger book belongs to:

_____

_____

_____

The Best Christmas Ever!

Marni McGee

Gavin Scott

LITTLE TIGER PRESS

London

Millicent Mouse was all a-flutter!
Christmas was only one day away,
and the little mouse could hardly wait.

She had swept and scrubbed until
everything sparkled. She had fluffed
and dusted until she sneezed.

STITCHOO!

Millicent gathered apples and nuts from the cellar.

BIG NUTS

BIGGER NUTS

EVEN BIGGER NUTS

Flour

In a flurry of flour, she baked an apple-nut pie.

She poured honey and spices into a kettle. Standing on tiptoe, she sniffed – and smiled.

"Christmas just WOULDN'T be Christmas," she said, "without my hot honey punch and apple-nut pie."

Millicent bundled up warm,
then scampered out into the snow.
Her black boots crunched as
she walked to and fro, gathering
lots and lots of ivy.

"Christmas just **wouldn't** be Christmas," she puffed, "**without** fresh ivy for my wreath and berries to string on my tree."

But instead of berries, Millicent found a
baby hedgehog, snoring softly in the snow.
"Witchety whiskers!"
she gasped and tiptoed close. "He needs
a better nest than that!"

So she wove all of her ivy into a leafy
blanket and gently tucked it around him.

By the time Millicent had finished, the sky was growing dark. "**Fiddle!**" she fussed. "Too late to search for berries now."

Millicent scurried home.

There she found Felicity Finch and her chicks, searching for food.

"What-oh-what shall we do?" the mother bird cried. "The snow has covered our seeds."

"Come in where it's warm," said Millicent. "I've just made an apple-nut pie."

In the flick of a wing, the kitchen was full
of hungry chicks. Their feathers fluttered and
flapped as they flocked around Millicent's pie.

To do...
- Clean
  dishes
- Wash floor
- Tidy the
  cupboards.

Shopping...
-Dusters
-Soap
-Furniture
 polish

"Tasty-tasty!
Kind, how kind!"

they chirped.

And then they were gone – in a whoosh
of feathers and dust. Millicent sneezed.
Stitchoo! Stitchoo!
Nothing was left but scattered crumbs.

Millicent heard a knock at the door. "**Fiddle!**" she muttered. "**Whatever now?**"

"Berry Chribbas, Billicent," called Gabriel Skunk. "I brogg you a bresent. Berfume."

"**Perfume!**" said Millicent, hiding a smile. "**Why, thank you.**" Gabriel dabbed at his nose. "I hab a tebbible code."

"Try my hot honey punch," she said. "It's very good for a terrible cold."

Gabriel lifted the kettle and drank every drop.

"Thaggs," he said and ambled off home.

Millicent looked all around. "It looks as if a storm has hit! Every dish is dirty. My pie and my punch are gobbled and gone. I have no ivy for my wreath, no berries for my tree. Witchety whiskers!

presents

- Mend chair
- Sew on patches.

- Gather wood
- Sort nuts
- Sweep up
- Dust rooms

HOW can Christmas be Christmas NOW?"

Then Millicent smiled. "At least I have my berfume...Perfume from a skunk!" she giggled, and bustled off to bed. "The baby hedgehog is **warm**," she whispered. "The chicks are **full** of pie, and the punch will **help** dear Gabriel's cold."

And with a yawn she fell asleep.

The next morning, Millicent woke to a chorus of cheeps and chirps. Outside were robins, sparrows and finches, and they were all singing – for her!

Behind the birds came a family of hedgehogs. Grandfather Hedgehog carried a sack, and the baby had flowers stuck in his prickly spines.

Cheepy-cheep!

Chirp!

Cheepy-cheep!

Last came Gabriel Skunk – with a
lopsided grin and a great big cake!
"**Gracious goodness!**"
exclaimed Millicent. She invited them in.

They trimmed the tree together with treasures
from Grandfather Hedgehog's sack – buttons
and ribbons, sparkling foil,
and scraps of cloth.

Millicent's black eyes sparkled. "This is the very **best Christmas ever!** And I am surely the happiest mouse in the forest. Christmas just couldn't be Christmas without my **wonderful friends!**"

Enjoy your best Christmas ever
with these fabulous books . . .

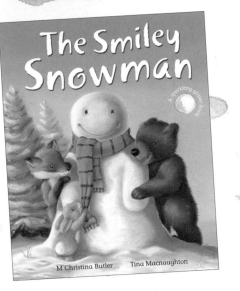

The Smiley Snowman

M Christina Butler   Tina Macnaughton

Silent Night

Juliet Groom
Tim Warnes

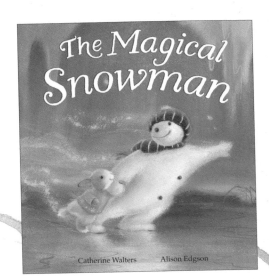

The Magical Snowman

Catherine Walters   Alison Edgson

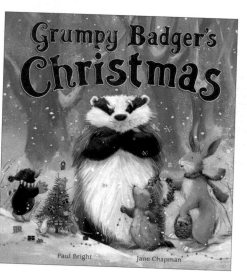

Grumpy Badger's Christmas

Paul Bright   Jane Chapman

The First Snow

M Christina Butler
Frank Endersby

Ten Christmas Wishes

Claire Freedman   Gail Yerrill

For information regarding any of the
above titles or for our catalogue, please contact us:
Little Tiger Press, 1 The Coda Centre, 189 Munster Road, London SW6 6AW
Tel: 020 7385 6333 • Fax: 020 7385 7333 • E-mail: info@littletiger.co.uk
www.littletigerpress.com

To Teddy and Max xx – LR

For Heston and Porter – MB

Published in the UK by Scholastic, 2022
1 London Bridge, London, SE1 9BA
Scholastic Ireland, 89E Lagan Road, Dublin Industrial Estate,
Glasnevin, Dublin, D11 HP5F

SCHOLASTIC and associated logos are trademarks and/or
registered trademarks of Scholastic Inc.

Text © Lucy Rowland, 2022
Illustrations © Mike Byrne, 2022

The right of Lucy Rowland and Mike Byrne to be identified
as the author and illustrator of this work has been asserted by them
under the Copyright, Designs and Patents Act 1988.

PB ISBN 978 0702 31023 2

A CIP catalogue record for this book is available from the British Library.

Printed in Italy
Paper made from wood grown in sustainable forests and other controlled sources

1 3 5 7 9 10 8 6 4 2

www.scholastic.co.uk

FSC
www.fsc.org
MIX
Paper from
responsible sources
FSC® C023419

Who Did a Wee? Wait and See!

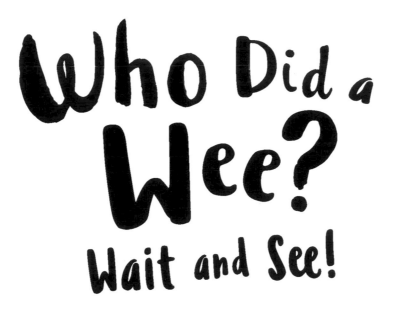

Lucy Rowland   Mike Byrne

■SCHOLASTIC

This morning, I got in a terrible muddle.

I walked in the kitchen and stepped in a puddle.

A puddle quite yellow. Oh no! Could it be?

A puddle I'm ever so certain was **WEE!**

But WHO could have left us this
puddle of piddle?
I knew what to do:
yes, I **MUST** solve the riddle!

Perhaps a **big** dinosaur popped in for tea
and felt rather **DESPERATE** to have a quick **wee**.

But, where was the bathroom?
She couldn't be sure
so let out some **wee**
(and an almighty **ROAR**)!

Or maybe a **princess** was dressed to impress.
She **raced** to the loo in her puffy pink dress,
but all of those layers were tricky, you see.

Her poor Royal Highness . . .

just **needed**
to pee!

Or maybe a **tiger** came round for a **prowl.**
He drank **all** our milk then he started to

growl.

Do **tigers** have manners? I'm sorry, not many,
and certainly not when they're **spending a penny!**

So maybe a **hero** swooped in from the sky

to **guzzle** some juice (with a slice of hot pie).

But then . . .
a full feeling.
He couldn't mistake it,
he needed a **wee**
but
he didn't
quite
make it!

Perhaps a big **shark** swam inside for some lunch and bathed in the **sink** while he had a good munch.

But on his way out, like a **wriggly worm,**

he **wiggled** and **jiggled** and started to **squirm.**

Or . . . yes, a small **bunny**, she came with her eggs.

She **hopped**

and she **jumped**

on her **strong** bunny legs.

But then, **whoops-a-daisy,** a feeling down low,
she did try to hold it but just **had** to go.

Or maybe a **witch**, *ZOOMING* past on her **broom**, decided to stop here and use the bathroom.

She'd drunk a **big** bottle
of funny green potion
and now she was BURSTING,
as full as the ocean!

Or maybe a **unicorn** leapt through the door and **sprinkled** his magic all over the floor?

A **twinkly tinkle** that **puddle** would be!
But no, this one looked just like **regular wee**.

So, if not the **witch**, or the loud **dinosaur**,
WHO crept in our kitchen and **weed** on the floor?

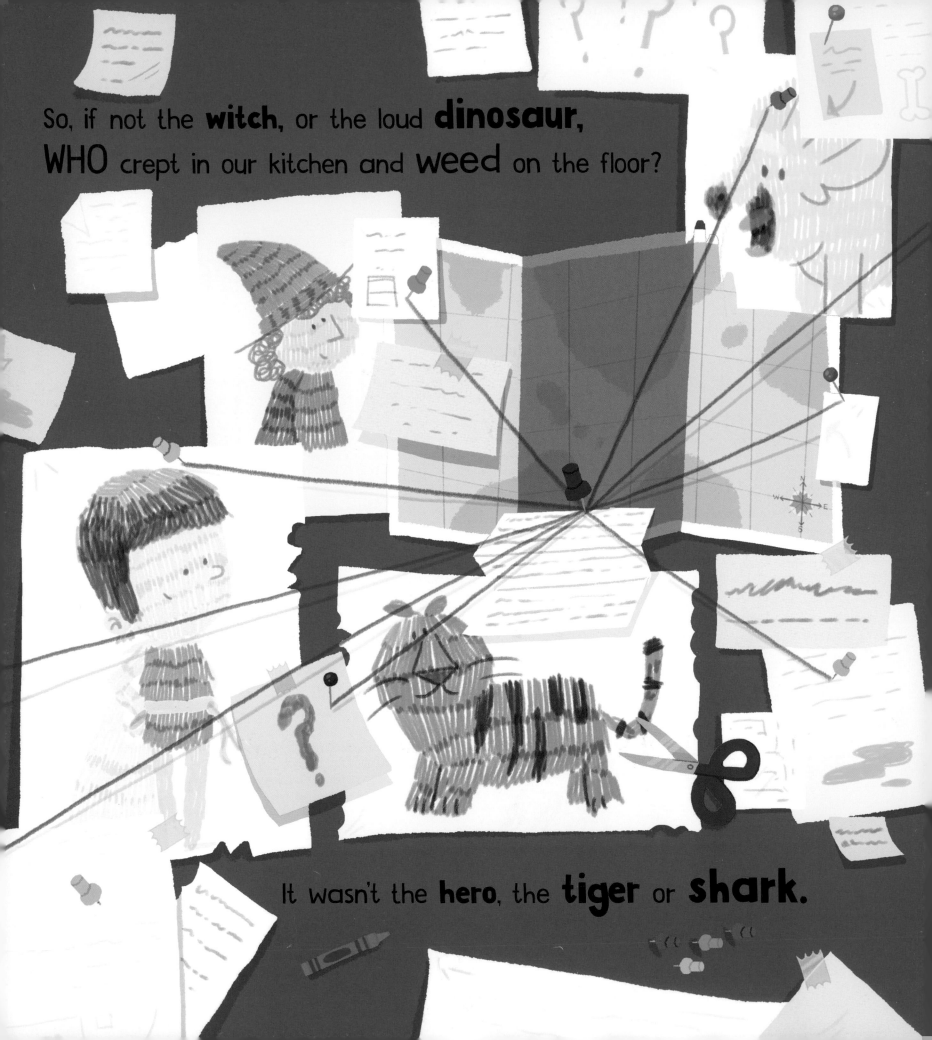

It wasn't the **hero**, the **tiger** or **shark**.

And **that's** when I **heard** it - a tiny, soft . . .

. . . BARK!

Our **puppy**, of course! She's still doing her training.
She's only a **baby**, so I'm not complaining.
We'll **hug** her and **pat** her and give her a **treat**,
and soon she'll go **wee-wee** outside in the street.

Our puppy will get there.
She gives a small yelp . . .

For, now we've got **plenty** of **pup-training** help!